The purchase of this item was
made possible by Collection
money award by
the 2007 Nevada Legislature

A Beginning-to-Read Book

The Witch Who Went for a Walk

by Margaret Hillert
Illustrated by Krystyna Stasiak

DEAR CAREGIVER, The *Beginning-to-Read* series is a carefully written collection of classic readers you may remember from your own childhood. Each book features text comprised of common sight words to provide your child ample practice reading the words that appear most frequently in written text. The many additional details in the pictures enhance the story and offer the opportunity for you to help your child expand oral language and develop comprehension.

Begin by reading the story to your child, followed by letting him or her read familiar words and soon your child will be able to read the story independently. At each step of the way, be sure to praise your reader's efforts to build his or her confidence as an independent reader. Discuss the pictures and encourage your child to make connections between the story and his or her own life. At the end of the story, you will find reading activities and a word list that will help your child practice and strengthen beginning reading skills.

Above all, the most important part of the reading experience is to have fun and enjoy it!

Shannon Cannon

Shannon Cannon,
Literacy Consultant

Norwood House Press • P.O. Box 316598 • Chicago, Illinois 60631
For more information about Norwood House Press please visit our website at
www.norwoodhousepress.com or call 866-565-2900.

LIBRARY OF CONGRESS CATALOGING-IN-PUBLICATION DATA
Hillert, Margaret.
   The witch who went for a walk / Margaret Hillert ; illustrated by Krystyna
Stasiak.
      p. cm. — (Beginning-to-read—revised and expanded)
   Originally published by Follett Publishing Company in 1981.
   Summary: "While taking a walk on Halloween night, a witch and her cat are
frightened by three children in costumes"—Provided by publisher.
   ISBN-13: 978-1-59953-186-1 (library edition : alk. paper)
   ISBN-10: 1-59953-186-0 (library edition : alk. paper) [1.
Witches—Fiction. 2. Halloween—Fiction.] I. Stasiak, Krystyna, ill. II.
Title.
   PZ7.H558Wi 2008
   [E]—dc22
                                         2008001668

Here I am.
Up, up, up.
Way up here.
See how I ride.

And see my cat.
He rides, too.
He is a good cat.
He helps me see.

We like it up here.
It is fun to ride up here.
We can look down.
Down, down, down.

It is fun up here.
But I want to go for a walk.
I guess I will go down
and have a look.

Here we are, cat.
Do you want to eat?
I will make you something
good to eat.

9

Now we will go for
a little walk.
Come on.
Come this way to see what we
can see.

Oh, oh.
What have we here?
Do you see what I see?
This is funny.

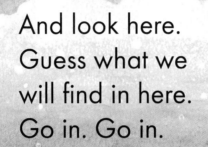

And look here.
Guess what we
will find in here.
Go in. Go in.

Look up, up, up.
See what is up there.
Something little.
Do you see that?

Now come out.
Walk, walk, walk.
I see something here, too.

I see friends.
One, two, three friends.
Oh, this is good.
I like to see friends.

But what is this?
Is it a friend?
No, no.
It is something funny.

It can not run.
It can not jump.
It sits and sits and sits.

I see something.
It looks like a cat.
It looks something like you.
What is it?

What are you?
I guess you are a cat.
But you are yellow!
My cat is not yellow.
You look funny.

I like this walk.
We look and look.
We have fun.

22

Now here is something.
Up here. Up here.
Who? Who?
Who are you?

O-o-o-o-h!
Look. Look.
Oh, my. Oh, my.
What is this?

E-e-e-e-e-e!
What is this?
I do not like this.
I do not like the way
you look.

27

No, no.
I do not like this.
Come away, cat. Come away.
We will have to go now.

Here we go.
Up, up, and away.
I guess a walk is not too
good for us.
This is the way to go.

The following activities support the findings of the National Reading Panel that determined the most effective components for reading instruction are: Phonemic Awareness, Phonics, Vocabulary, Fluency, and Text Comprehension.

Phonemic Awareness: The /w/ and /hw/ sounds

Oral Blending: Say the following words and ask your child to repeat the beginning sound in each word after you say it: walk, want, way, we, what, will. The word **what** should sound slightly different from the other words. The sound at the beginning is /**hw**/.

Say the word parts on the left to your child. Ask your child to repeat the word, adding the /**w**/ or /**hw**/ sound to the beginning:

ag = wag	in = win	ire = wire	ill = will
e = we	est = west	aste = waste	ave = wave

Phonics: The letters Ww and Hh

1. Demonstrate how to form the letters **W** and **w** for your child.

2. Have your child practice writing **W** and **w** at least three times each.

3. Ask your child to point to the words in the book that begin with the letter **Ww**.

4. Demonstrate how to form the letters **H** and **h** for your child.

5. Have your child practice writing **H** and **h** at least three times each.

6. Ask your child to point to the words in the book that begin with the letter **Hh**.

7. Explain to your child that the letters **w** and **h** sometimes make the /**hw**/ sound. Say the words **weather** and **whether**. The beginning sound is only slightly different, and often the two beginning sounds sound the same.

8. Write down the following words with the spaces representing missing letters. Ask your child to fill in the spaces by writing the letters **wh** in them. Ask your child to read each word aloud.

__ere	__ale	__ip	__eel	__en
__ite	__isper	__y	__ich	

Vocabulary: Verb Tense

1. Explain to your child that action words can be either present tense, past tense, or future tense. Present tense means it is happening right now, past tense means that it already happened, and future tense means that it will happen eventually.

2. Write each of the following story words on separate index cards: go, see, ride, are, were, come, have, find, is, run. For each word, ask your child to provide the past tense and future tense verb forms and write them on separate index cards.

3. Mix up the index cards and ask your child to match the present, past, and future tense verbs.

Fluency: Choral Reading

1. Reread the story with your child at least two more times while your child tracks the print by running a finger under the words as they are read. Ask your child to read the words he or she knows with you.

2. Reread the story aloud together. Be careful to read at a rate that your child can keep up with.

3. Repeat choral reading and allow your child to be the lead reader. Ask him or her to change from a whisper to a loud voice while you follow along and change your voice.

Text Comprehension: Discussion Time

1. Ask your child to retell the sequence of events in the story.

2. To check comprehension, ask your child the following questions:

   - What are some of the things the witch sees in the story?

   - Why is the witch surprised by the yellow cat?

   - Why did the witch fly away on her broom?

   - If you dress up on Halloween, describe your favorite costume.

WORD LIST

The Witch Who Went for a Walk **uses the 67 words listed below.**
This list can be used to practice reading the words that appear in the text.
You may wish to write the words on index cards and use them to help your
child build automatic word recognition. Regular practice with these words
will enhance your child's fluency in reading connected text.

a	find	jump	ride(s)	walk
am	for		run	want
and	friend(s)	like		way
are	fun	little	see	we
away	funny	look(s)	sits	what
			something	who
but	go	make		will
	good	me	that	
can	guess	my	the	yellow
cat			there	you
come	have	no	this	
	he	not	three	
do	helps	now	to	
down	here		too	
	how	oh	two	
eat		on		
	I	one	up	
	in	out	us	
	is			
	it			

ABOUT THE AUTHOR Margaret Hillert has written over 80 books for children who are just learning to read. Her books have been translated into many different languages and over a million children throughout the world have read her books. She first started writing poetry as a child and has continued to write for children and adults throughout her life. A first grade teacher for 34 years, Margaret is now retired from teaching and lives in Michigan where she likes to write, take walks in the morning, and care for her three cats.

Photograph by Glenna Washburn

ABOUT THE ADVISER Shannon Cannon contributed the activities pages that appear in this book. Shannon serves as a literacy consultant and provides staff development to help improve reading instruction. She is a frequent presenter at educational conferences and workshops. Prior to this she worked as an elementary school teacher and as president of a curriculum publishing company.